Abrams Books for Young Readers • New York

CACTUS and FLOWER

A BOOK ABOUT LIFE CYCLES

SARAH
WILLIAMSON

Cactus and Flower lived in the desert, side by side.

Together, they watched the sun come up.

And together, they watched the sun go down . . .

. . . and the sky turn from yellow

to orange

to blue

to purple

to pink

to red.

They spent many days together.
"Butterfly days" were what they called them.

Once in a while,
everyone came out to play.

Each night they played a game where they found different friends in the sky.

"My stars," Flower would always say.

Cactus grew taller, slowly but surely.

And Flower grew, too. Such is life.

One day, Flower lost a petal.

Poof.

Just like that.

Cactus knew what this meant.
And Flower knew, too.

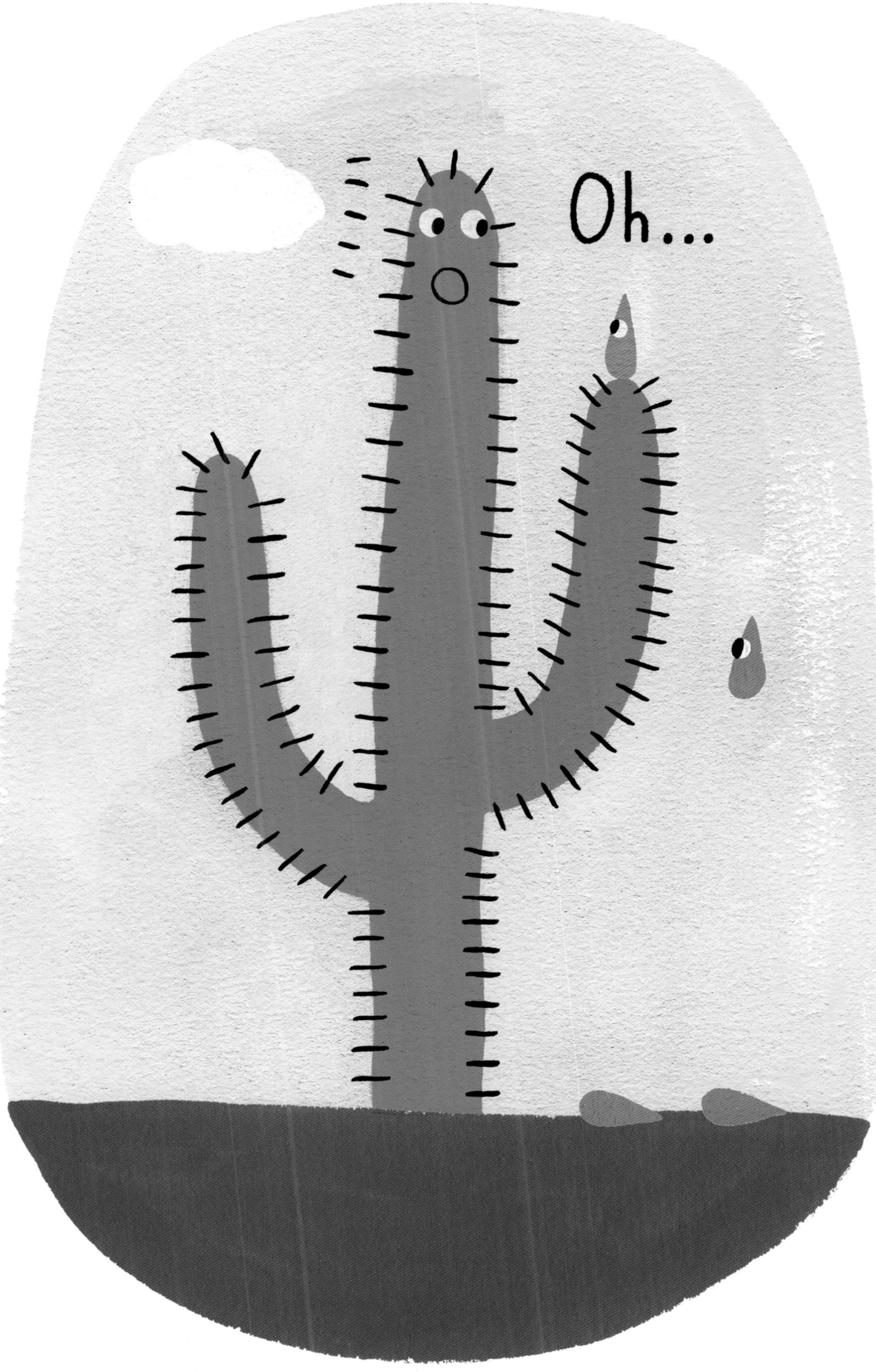
Oh...

Cactus's eyes were watery as
Flower's last petal blew away.

All the butterflies in the world
tried to cheer Cactus up.

Days passed.

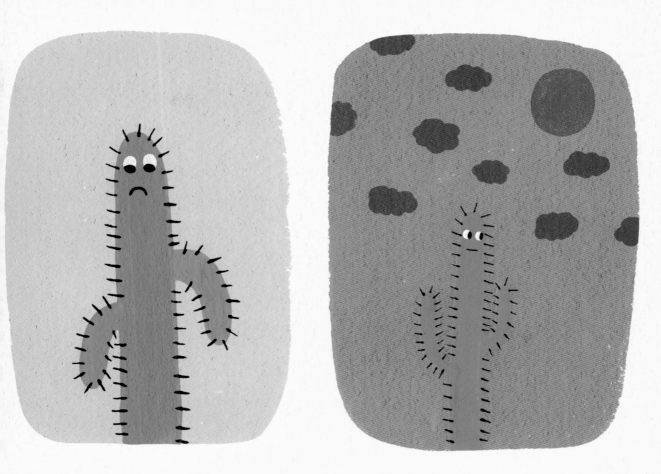

And days and more days.

Cactus watched the clouds go by.

At one point, he saw a cloud
that looked like Flower!

Cactus smiled at the
thought of his friend.

More time passed.
Then a little green bud appeared.

Cactus knew what this meant.
And, slowly but surely . . .

. . . there were butterfly days again.

A NOTE FROM THE AUTHOR

I have been visiting Tucson, Arizona, for the last fifteen years and am continually captivated by the spectacular desert. Many mornings, I wake up before dawn in order to watch the sky change colors. I have become enamored by the cacti and the flowers. Cacti come in different shapes and sizes, and each one, I can tell, has a unique personality.

There is also a natural life cycle element to be observed in the desert. The cacti, with their longer life spans, serve as strong and sturdy friends to the flowers, who come and go with the passing of time. This profundity is not lost on me.

—S.W.

TO CHRISTOPHER KREILING

The illustrations for this book were made with gouache.

Cataloging-in-Publication Data has been applied for and may be obtained from the Library of Congress.

ISBN 978-1-4197-4337-5

Text and illustrations copyright © 2020 Sarah Williamson
Book design by Steph Stilwell

Printed and bound in China
10 9 8 7 6 5 4 3 2 1

Abrams Books for Young Readers are available at special discounts when purchased in quantity for premiums and promotions as well as fundraising or educational use. Special editions can also be created to specification. For details, contact specialsales@abramsbooks.com or the address below.

Abrams® is a registered trademark of Harry N. Abrams, Inc.

ABRAMS The Art of Books
195 Broadway, New York, NY 10007
abramsbooks.com